PUMPKIN HILL

by **Elizabeth Spurr**

illustrated by **Whitney Martin**

Holiday House / New York

The artwork was created with acrylic paints on Arches 140 hot press paper.
The text typeface is Greco Roman.
www.holidayhouse.com
First Edition
1 3 5 7 9 10 8 6 4 2

Library of Congress Cataloging-in-Publication Data
Spurr. Elizabeth.
Pumpkin Hill / by Elizabeth Spurr : illustrated by Whitney Martin.— 1st ed.
p. cm.
Summary: The townspeople must decide what to do with thousands
of pumpkins that roll down a hill and into their midst just before Halloween.
ISBN 0-8234-1869-3 (hardcover)
[1. Pumpkin—Fiction. 2. Halloween—Fiction.] I. Martin. Whitney. 1968- ill. II. Title.
PZ7.S7695Pu 2006
[E]— dc22
2003068594

ISBN-13: 978-0-8234-1869-5
ISBN-10: 0-8234-1869-3

There once was a pumpkin,
a lonely only pumpkin
that grew on the brink of a great green hill.

The sun shone. The rain fell.
The pumpkin grew and grew,
larger and orangier, and plump, plump, plumper,
till one fine day it broke from its vine
and roly-polyed down the hill.
The pumpkin hit a stone,
and *KERSPLAT!* That was that.

Or was it?

The pumpkin seeds lay
on the soft, fertile earth,
which soon wore a blanket of snow.

In spring the farmer came
with his horse-drawn plow,
scattering the seeds
across the great green hill.

But he and his wife could not agree.
Barley or corn?
Alfalfa or hay?
So the hill was left unplanted
(except for the pumpkin seeds).

The rains came; the sun shone.
The seeds grew into sprouts,
the sprouts into vines,
vines with leaves,
leaves and flowers,
flowers into . . .
. . . roly-poly pumpkins!

But since no one came to pick them,
they withered away
(except for the pumpkin seeds).

In spring the farmer plowed once more.
"Tomatoes?"
"Potatoes!"
"Turnips?"
(His hill remained unplanted
except for the pumpkin seeds.)
Sun and rain. Once around again.
Sprouts, vines, roly-poly pumpkins,
which withered away . . . except for . . . !

Once again in spring the farmer plowed
but didn't sow.
Little did he know he had no need.
Beneath the soil a crop was widely planted—
those hardy little pumpkin seeds!
They grew in sun and rain.
from small green lumpkins
into round fat *plumpkins*.

Because the farmer lived
on the far side of the hill,
he did not see that the land
had turned a bright orange
with a mass of roly-poly pumpkins!

There came a mighty wind,
the whirly, swirly kind.
It blew the vines into a tangle
and sent the pumpkins rumble-tumble,
hurtling down the great green hill.

The valley town was wakened
by a roar as loud as thunder,
as thousands of pumpkins
thumped and bumped down the slope.
Behold, a golden avalanche!

Traffic jammed: shops shut.
What a delightful disaster!
The pumpkins bonked pedestrians
and ricocheted off walls.
They rolled into the marketplace
and tumbled all the vegetables
into a giant tossed salad!

Pumpkins rolled into canneries
and stalled conveyor belts.
Cried the workers, "This is more than
our cannery can can!"

One could not help but chuckle
to see uppity folk struggle
with those most unruly roly-polies.
Who could stay a grouchy grumpkin
among those jolly, bumping pumpkins?

The mayor called a meeting. "What shall we do
with this pre-pos-ter-ous pre-dom-i-nance of pumpkins?"
"Make jack-o'-lanterns," cried the children.
"Remember, it's almost Halloween!"

So the mayor decreed
that each citizen
must take home a pumpkin to carve.
But when all had claimed their share,
a pleth-o-ra of pumpkins
still lined the sides of the road.
The children cried, "Make pumpkin pies!"

All Hallows' Eve at moonrise,
the whole valley glowed
with the grins of six thousand jack-o'-lanterns.
The night air wafted the scent,
spicy and sweet,
of three thousand and five pumpkin pies.
Children dressed as ghosts and goblins
paraded on the green.
Each held a candled pumpkin.
What a blazing Halloween!

The farmer apologized for causing such a mess.
The frazzled mayor shouted, "No more pumpkins!"
The farmer and his wife
talked head-to-head.
Then he announced to the crowd,
"I'd like to set aside my great green hill
for all these children.
They can run here, they can hide.
Ski, slide, or pony ride.
They'll grow healthy, they'll grow tall
on this land that I will call
Pumpkin Hill."
"A pro-pi-tious solution," said the mayor,
"for our pumpkin pollution!"

Then the mayor imposed a harsh punishment
on anyone who scattered pumpkin seeds:
The guilty one must gobble fifteen pumpkin pies
within a quarter of an hour!

That is the reason why on Halloween,
after carving grim faces with fire-lit eyes,
children salt, roast, and eat, for supper or snack,
those per-ni-cious-ly prolific pumpkin seeds.

Grow a giant pumpkin!

Things you will need:
  pumpkin seeds
  4-inch flowerpots
  potting soil
  a sunny spot in a yard or garden
  compost or plant food
  a shingle, a crown of wire, or a piece of heavy plastic

1. In early May plant pumpkin seeds 1 inch deep in the flowerpots filled with potting soil.
2. When seedlings sprout, plant them outside 6–8 inches apart in a sunny place that faces south. Add compost or plant food to the soil.
3. As each plant grows, cut off all but two branches.
4. When flowers appear, take off all but one flower from each branch.
5. Cover the branches with mounds of soil so roots can form. Water as needed.
6. Place a shingle, a crown of wire, or a piece of heavy plastic under each pumpkin to protect it from damp soil.
7. Enjoy your giant pumpkins in the fall.

Roasted pumpkin seeds make a nourishing nibble.

Things you will need:
  an adult to help
  a pumpkin
  a knife
  a large spoon
  paper towels
  a cookie sheet
  vegetable oil

1. Have an adult open the pumpkin by cutting a large circle at the top with a knife.
2. Scoop out the seeds with the spoon.
3. Wash the seeds thoroughly under the faucet, then spread them on paper towels to dry.
4. Grease a cookie sheet with vegetable oil.
5. Scatter seeds over the cookie sheet.
6. Have an adult help you bake the seeds in a slow (250°F) oven for at least an hour, shaking them occasionally.
7. When the seeds are completely dried, turn the heat to 350°F for a few minutes to brown them slightly. Watch carefully! Remember to turn off the oven.
8. Let the seeds cool. Salt the seeds if you like, and store them in an airtight tin.